Monster for Hire

Published in the United States of America in 1994 by
MONDO Publishing

By arrangement with MULTIMEDIA INTERNATIONAL (UK) LTD

For information contact:
MONDO Publishing
980 Avenue of the Americas
New York, NY 10018
MONDO is a registered trademark of Mondo Publishing

Visit our website at www.mondopub.com

Printed in the China
First Mondo printing, October 1994
    11 12 13 14 PB 9 8 7 6
10 11 12 13 14 SP 9 8 7 6 5 4 3 2 1

ISBN 1-879531-61-5 (PB) 1-60175-624-0 (SP)

Originally published in Australia in 1987 by Horwitz Publications Pty Ltd
Original development by Snowball Educational

Library of Congress Cataloging-in-Publication Data
Wilson, Trevor
     Monster for Hire / written by Trevor Wilson ; illustrated by Regina Newey.
          p.   cm.
     Summary: After being fired by a giant and a prince, a monster manages
to outwit a sorcerer and make a cozy home for himself.
     [1. Monsters—Fiction.] L Newey, Regina, ill. II. Title.
PZ7.W6988Mo   1994
[Fic]—dc20   94-28976
                                                                          CIP
                                                                           AC

Monster for Hire

Written by Trevor Wilson   Illustrated by Regina Newey

MONDO

On a stony hill between two towns lived a giant. Because he was often away the giant decided to hire a monster to guard his castle. So he put a sign on the castle wall.

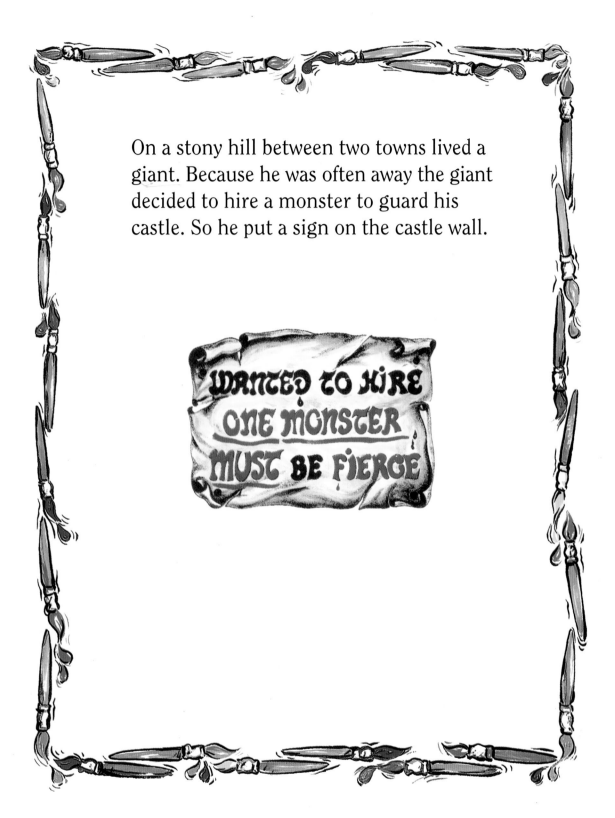

WANTED TO HIRE
ONE MONSTER
MUST BE FIERCE

Along came a monster. "I'm looking for work," he said. "Try me."

"Are you fierce?" asked the giant.

"Very!" the monster assured him. He screwed up his face and growled his fiercest growl.

"Hmmph," grunted the giant, not impressed. "That looked more like a toothache to me, but I suppose you'll do."

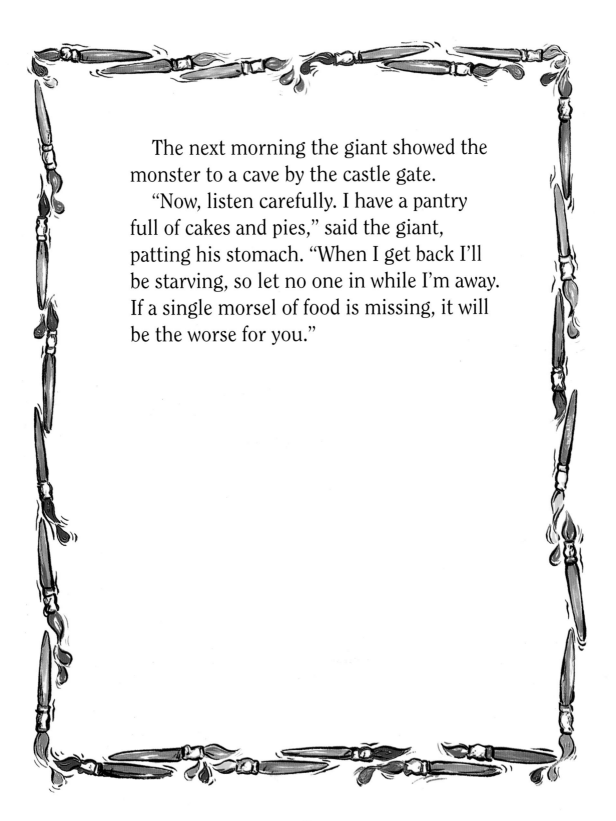

The next morning the giant showed the monster to a cave by the castle gate.

"Now, listen carefully. I have a pantry full of cakes and pies," said the giant, patting his stomach. "When I get back I'll be starving, so let no one in while I'm away. If a single morsel of food is missing, it will be the worse for you."

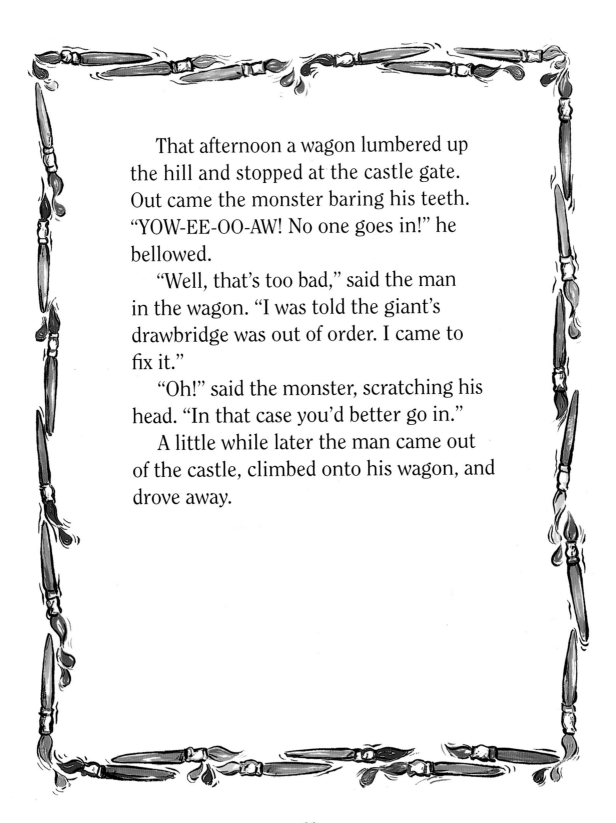

That afternoon a wagon lumbered up
the hill and stopped at the castle gate.
Out came the monster baring his teeth.
"YOW-EE-OO-AW! No one goes in!" he
bellowed.

"Well, that's too bad," said the man
in the wagon. "I was told the giant's
drawbridge was out of order. I came to
fix it."

"Oh!" said the monster, scratching his
head. "In that case you'd better go in."

A little while later the man came out
of the castle, climbed onto his wagon, and
drove away.

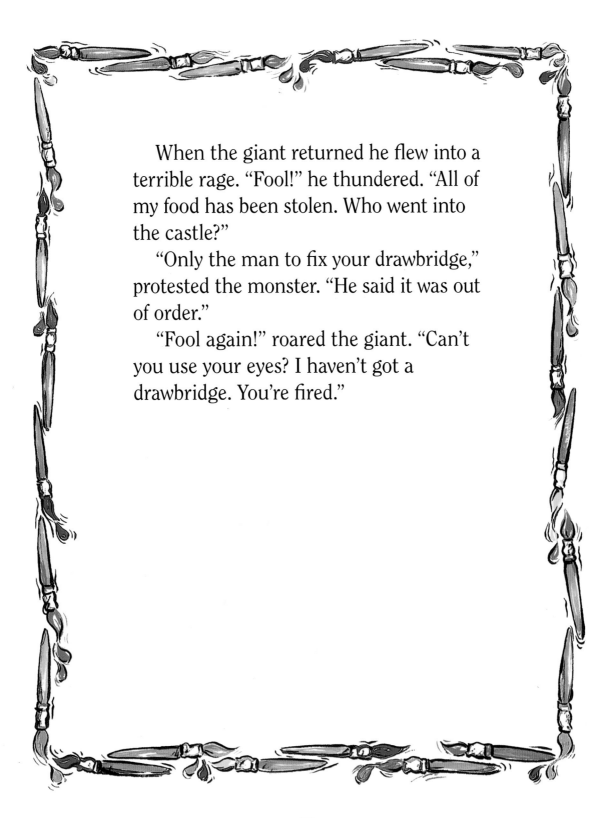

When the giant returned he flew into a terrible rage. "Fool!" he thundered. "All of my food has been stolen. Who went into the castle?"

"Only the man to fix your drawbridge," protested the monster. "He said it was out of order."

"Fool again!" roared the giant. "Can't you use your eyes? I haven't got a drawbridge. You're fired."

So the giant put another sign on the castle wall.

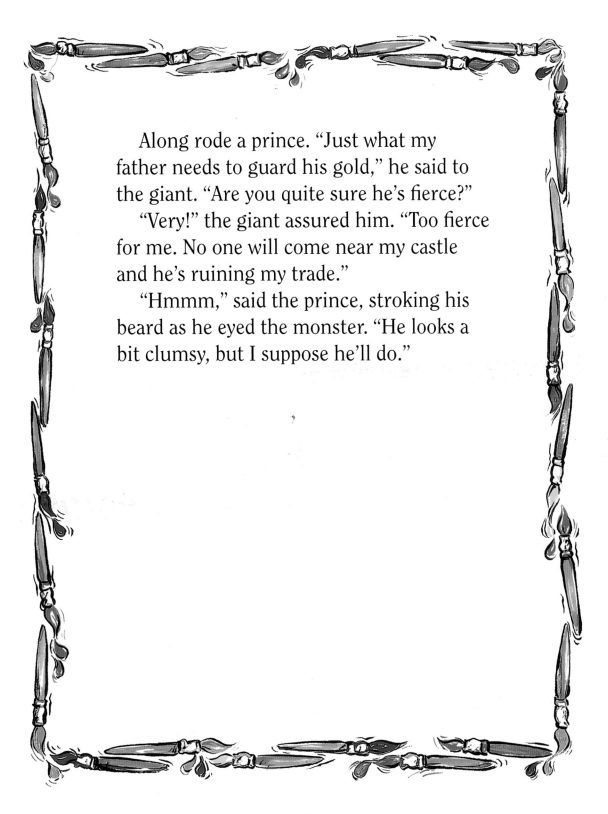

Along rode a prince. "Just what my father needs to guard his gold," he said to the giant. "Are you quite sure he's fierce?"

"Very!" the giant assured him. "Too fierce for me. No one will come near my castle and he's ruining my trade."

"Hmmm," said the prince, stroking his beard as he eyed the monster. "He looks a bit clumsy, but I suppose he'll do."

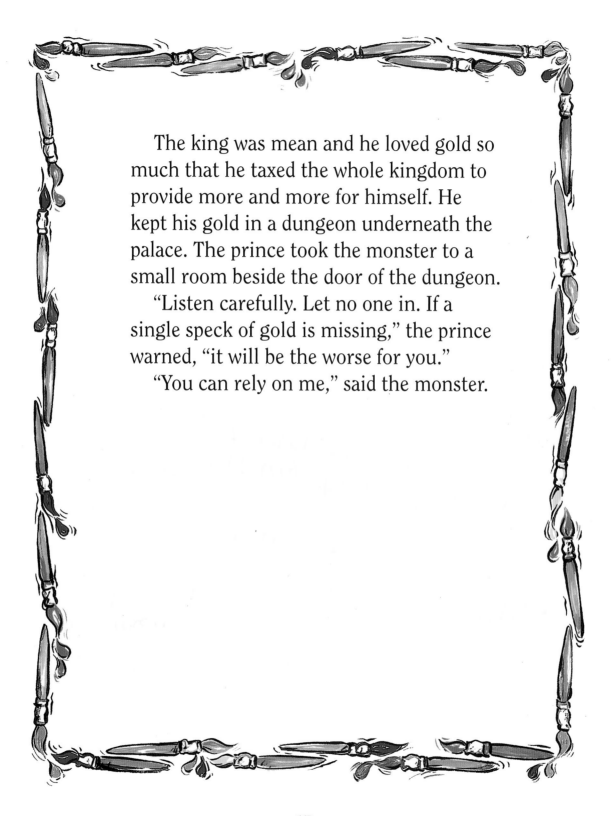

The king was mean and he loved gold so much that he taxed the whole kingdom to provide more and more for himself. He kept his gold in a dungeon underneath the palace. The prince took the monster to a small room beside the door of the dungeon.

"Listen carefully. Let no one in. If a single speck of gold is missing," the prince warned, "it will be the worse for you."

"You can rely on me," said the monster.

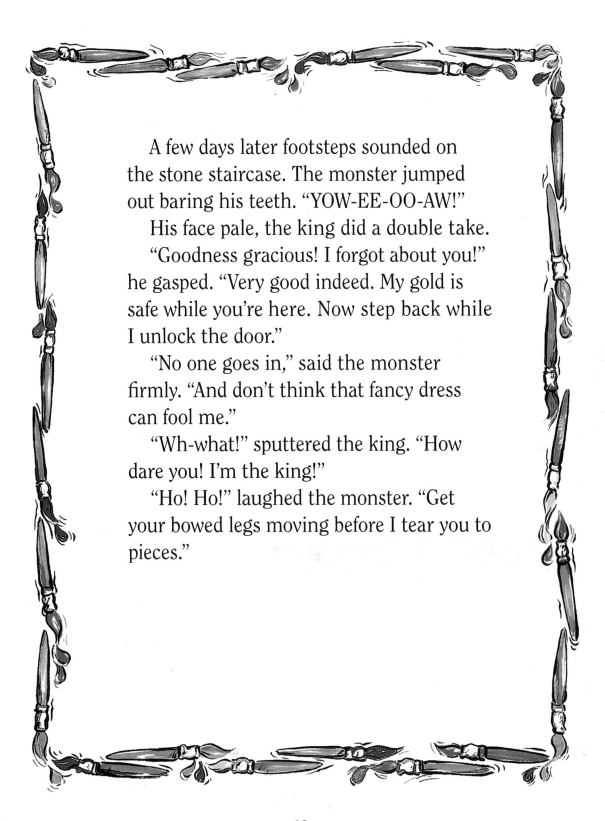

A few days later footsteps sounded on the stone staircase. The monster jumped out baring his teeth. "YOW-EE-OO-AW!"

His face pale, the king did a double take.

"Goodness gracious! I forgot about you!" he gasped. "Very good indeed. My gold is safe while you're here. Now step back while I unlock the door."

"No one goes in," said the monster firmly. "And don't think that fancy dress can fool me."

"Wh-what!" sputtered the king. "How dare you! I'm the king!"

"Ho! Ho!" laughed the monster. "Get your bowed legs moving before I tear you to pieces."

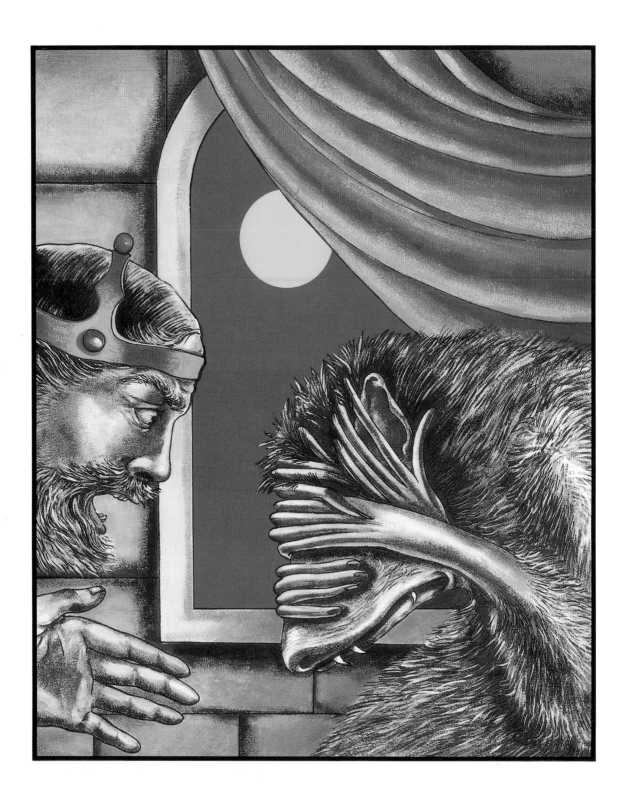

Purple with rage, the king turned and stormed back up the staircase. Soon afterwards the prince hurried down. He was in a fine temper.

"Fool! Dolt! Imbecile!" he cried. "You have insulted the king. You'll have to go."

So a sign was hung on the palace wall.

A sorcerer came by. After reading the sign, the sorcerer knocked on the palace gate.

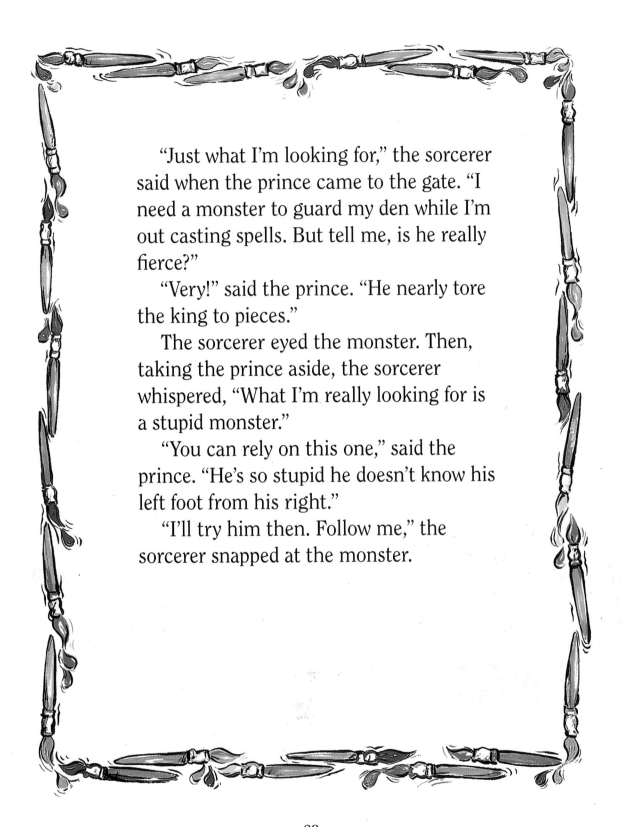

"Just what I'm looking for," the sorcerer said when the prince came to the gate. "I need a monster to guard my den while I'm out casting spells. But tell me, is he really fierce?"

"Very!" said the prince. "He nearly tore the king to pieces."

The sorcerer eyed the monster. Then, taking the prince aside, the sorcerer whispered, "What I'm really looking for is a stupid monster."

"You can rely on this one," said the prince. "He's so stupid he doesn't know his left foot from his right."

"I'll try him then. Follow me," the sorcerer snapped at the monster.

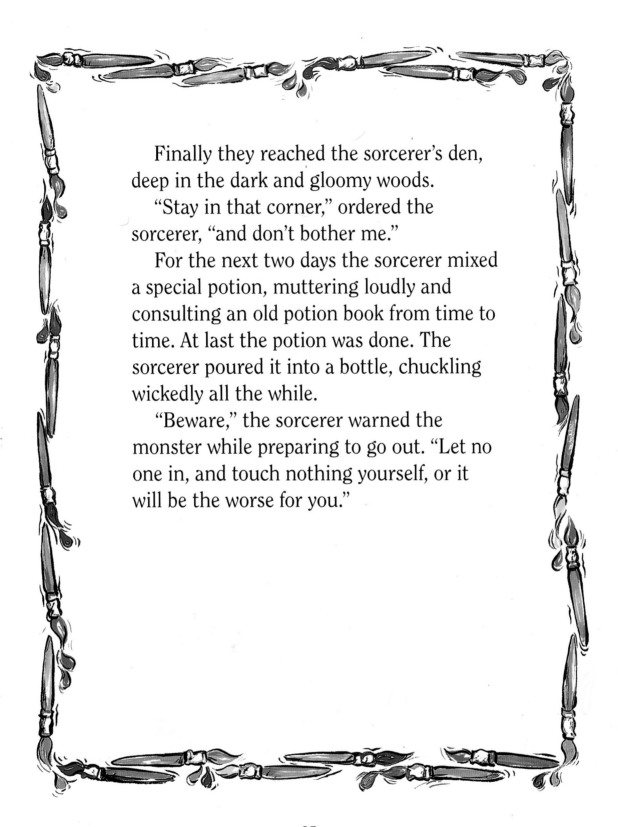

Finally they reached the sorcerer's den, deep in the dark and gloomy woods.

"Stay in that corner," ordered the sorcerer, "and don't bother me."

For the next two days the sorcerer mixed a special potion, muttering loudly and consulting an old potion book from time to time. At last the potion was done. The sorcerer poured it into a bottle, chuckling wickedly all the while.

"Beware," the sorcerer warned the monster while preparing to go out. "Let no one in, and touch nothing yourself, or it will be the worse for you."

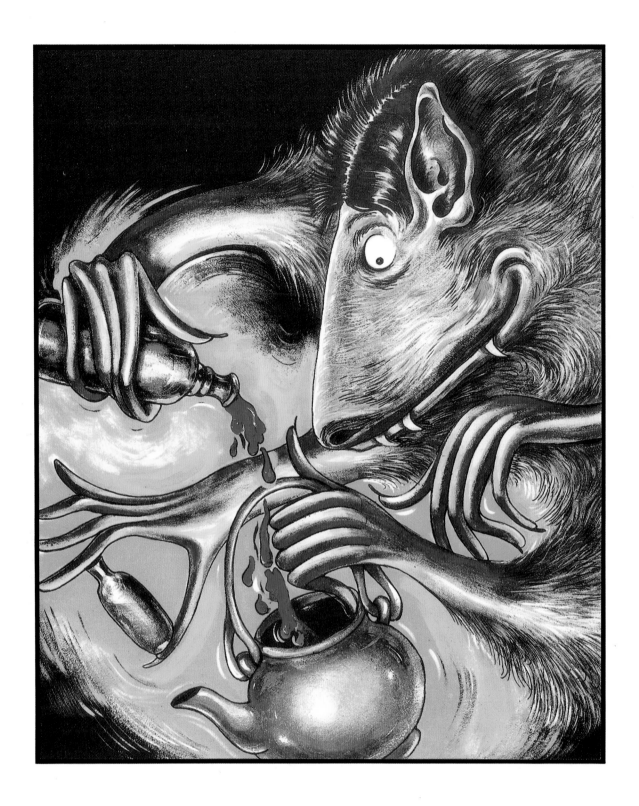

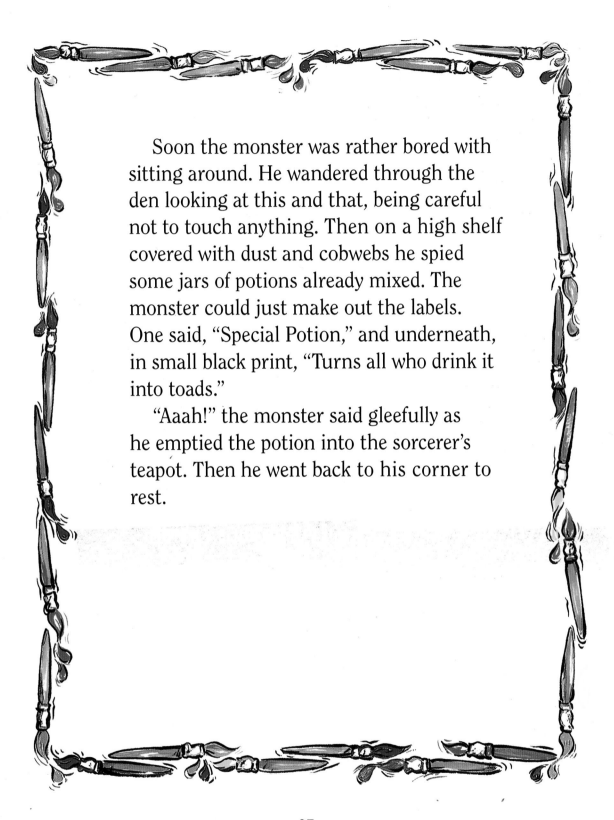

Soon the monster was rather bored with sitting around. He wandered through the den looking at this and that, being careful not to touch anything. Then on a high shelf covered with dust and cobwebs he spied some jars of potions already mixed. The monster could just make out the labels. One said, "Special Potion," and underneath, in small black print, "Turns all who drink it into toads."

"Aaah!" the monster said gleefully as he emptied the potion into the sorcerer's teapot. Then he went back to his corner to rest.

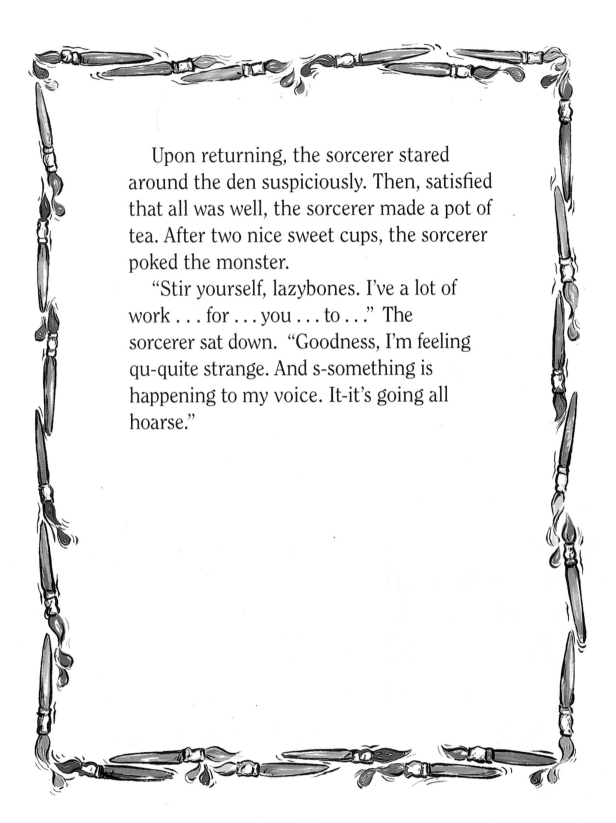

Upon returning, the sorcerer stared around the den suspiciously. Then, satisfied that all was well, the sorcerer made a pot of tea. After two nice sweet cups, the sorcerer poked the monster.

"Stir yourself, lazybones. I've a lot of work . . . for . . . you . . . to . . ." The sorcerer sat down. "Goodness, I'm feeling qu-quite strange. And s-something is happening to my voice. It-it's going all hoarse."

And without further ado the sorcerer changed into a very odd-looking creature indeed. "Arrk! Arrk!" croaked the creature as it hopped off to the nearest pond.

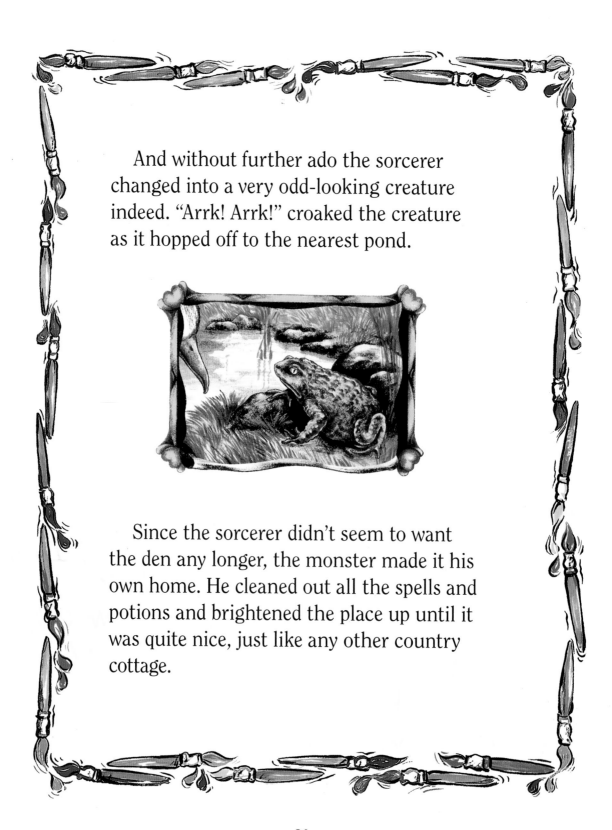

Since the sorcerer didn't seem to want the den any longer, the monster made it his own home. He cleaned out all the spells and potions and brightened the place up until it was quite nice, just like any other country cottage.

And he put a sign on the cottage door.